YELLOW BLUE JAY

Jay stood in the doorway. Outside it was very dark. Of course there were no streetlights. There were no streets. As Jay's eyes adjusted he could make out the shapes of the bushes around the house and the trees. What was hiding behind the bushes?

Mickey pulled Jay by the arm. "Come on, Yellow Blue Jay," he said.

As his bare foot touched the ground, Jay suddenly had an amazing thought. He had never been outdoors at night without an adult before. There was a sound in the bushes to the right of the house. Jay stood absolutely still. He couldn't have run even if Mickey let go of his arm.

"That's the bear." whispered Mickey. "Shine the light over there."

Shivering, Jay moved the flashlight to shine in that direction. The light bobbed up and down. His teeth chattered. What kind of teeth did a bear have? he wondered. Probably very sharp ones.

YELLOW BLUE JAY

YELLOW BLUE JAY

Johanna Hurwitz

Illustrated by Donald Carrick

A Beech Tree Paperback Book

New York

3 5 7 9 8 6 4 2

Library of Congress Cataloging-in-Publication Data

Hurwitz, Johanna.
    Yellow blue jay / Johanna Hurwitz ; illustrated by Donald Carrick.
— 1st Beech Tree ed.
     p.   cm.
    Summary: Happy to spend his summer vacation at home in the city,
eight-year-old Jay is horrified by his parents' plan to spend two
weeks in the Vermont woods sharing a house with another family.
    ISBN 0-688-12278-7
    [1. Country life—Fiction. 2. Vermont—Fiction. 3. Self
-confidence—Fiction. 4. Friendship—Fiction.] I. Carrick,
Donald, ill. II. Title.
[PZ7.H9574Ye   1993]
[Fic]—dc20
                                            92-24597
                                              CIP
                                              AC

For Uri, Nomi, and Beni
Remembering summers on Snow Vidda

·Contents·

YELLOW BLUE JAY

· 1 ·

· Off to the Woods ·

From the backseat of his parents' car, Jay Koota looked longingly at the apartment building where his family lived. It was August and the Kootas were about to leave for two weeks in Vermont. Jay had never been to Vermont and he didn't want to go. He did not like new places and new things. He was happiest when every day was exactly like the day before.

In school his third-grade classmates had begun a countdown immediately after Memorial Day. Everyone checked off the days until school was over. Jay thought he was the only boy in all of New York—all the world probably—who didn't look forward to summer vacation. He preferred school. He liked knowing that every morning he would sit in the same seat, see the same teacher, follow the same pattern. He even liked school lunches: sloppy joes and canned string beans, fish sticks and soft spaghetti, and his favorite, macaroni and cheese.

One reason Jay didn't like summer was day camp. Last summer his parents had insisted upon enrolling him. He had hated it—all the kids, the running around, the swimming lessons. Everyday he'd come home sweaty and dirty and grumpy. This year he had gone again. At least, he thought he would know what to expect. But he had been wrong. There were new counselors and new kids. He suffered through more embarrassing swimming lessons and noisy volleyball games. There had been a camp play, and Jay was in the chorus. He had to wear a long white robe that itched around the neck and made him sweat.

As if day camp was not bad enough, his parents had rented a house in the woods of Vermont, sight unseen. Mrs. Koota had read an ad in the newspaper and showed it to Mr. Koota.

Jay hoped his father wouldn't want to go. He had been looking forward to spending the days between the end of camp and the beginning of fourth grade at home. He liked to build models and he had been saving for one that he knew would take a long time to build.

"Sounds great," said Mr. Koota. "Let's take it."

Jay's sister Ellen, who was six, jumped up and down with excitement while Mrs. Koota made all the arrangements. She was too young to know how boring it would be, thought Jay.

The newspaper had said the house in the woods slept twelve.

"Imagine that!" Mrs. Koota had mused, and two long-distance phone calls later, they were sharing the house with Mrs. Koota's college roommate and her family. The Rosses lived in Ohio, and Jay's mother hadn't seen Mrs. Ross in seven years. Since Jay was eight, he didn't remember meeting the Ross family when they visited New York seven years ago.

The Rosses had two children, Mickey, who was twelve, and Stacey, who was seven. Mrs. Koota and Mrs. Ross kept in touch through letters.

"I don't remember them," Jay complained.

"You cried the entire time," Mrs. Koota recalled. "You were teething."

"What about me?" asked Ellen.

"You weren't even born seven years ago."

"That's not fair," Ellen whined, as she did several times every day.

Jay didn't say anything then. But now, sitting in the back of the car, he thought Ellen was right. It was not fair to have to go to this strange house and stay with strange people. When he grew up, he would spend every day of his vacations in an air-conditioned movie theater with a giant box of popcorn in his lap. Buttered.

Mrs. Koota turned around and smiled at Jay.

"You're going to have a wonderful time with Mickey," she said.

Jay didn't answer. His mother meant well. But he knew that no twelve-year-old boy would want to play with him. It would be awful for Mickey and awful for him, but, he was fairly certain it would be more awful for him. It usually was.

"We're off," said Mr. Koota as the car pulled out into the street.

"We're off!" shouted Ellen.

The drive to Vermont would take six hours, including a stop along the way for a meal. But less than twenty minutes after the car had left the city, Jay found his eyelids closing and in twenty-two minutes, he was sound asleep.

Jay woke up to eat and then slept again. It was late afternoon when they reached the house. "We're here. We're here," Ellen shouted in his ear.

Groggily Jay opened his eyes. All around him were trees and more trees. In the distance he could see a mountain. And in front of them was a lone house without a number. Jay wondered how his parents found this unmarked house on this unpaved road. Maybe this wasn't the right house, he thought.

Everyone got out of the car.

"Wait," called Mr. Koota as his wife went to open the door of the house. "Let's take a picture of everyone outside."

Jay sighed. His father was always making them pose for pictures. Mrs. Koota stood in the center with Ellen on one side and Jay on the other.

"Smile," said Mr. Koota as he focused the camera.

"X-Y-Z," Mrs. Koota whispered in her son's ear.

"You're supposed to say 'cheese,' " he corrected her.

"X-Y-Z," she said. "Examine your zipper." Jay sighed. His buttons were always popping open or off, and his zippers didn't stay up either. His mother said he had baby fat. Jay bent to adjust his zipper and his father said, "Jay! You're not looking at the camera. Stand still, everyone."

Jay fixed his zipper and Mr. Koota took a picture. "There was no one here to notice," he said.

"Maybe there are bears!" said Ellen. "Bears live in the woods, don't they?"

"Not these woods," said Mr. Koota, putting his camera back inside its case.

"That's not fair," said Ellen.

"We beat the Rosses getting here," Mrs. Koota called from the doorway of the house. "Their trip is much longer than ours." The key that she had gotten in the mail had opened the front door. It was the right house, Jay noted as he followed the others inside. He wasn't in any hurry. The house wasn't going to run away.

"Where am I going to sleep?" Ellen demanded.

On the ground floor were two bedrooms, a bathroom, a large living room-dining room, and a kitchen built into one wall. Downstairs there was another bathroom and two more bedrooms. Each of these rooms held two bunk beds.

"How shall we arrange it? By family? Or boys in one room and girls in another?" asked Mrs. Koota.

It had never occurred to Jay that he might

have to share a room with Mickey Ross. "I think families should stick together," he told his mother quickly.

"I want to sleep on top," said Ellen. She had already climbed the ladder and was bouncing on an upper bunk.

"Each child can have a top bunk," said Mrs. Koota. "There are four."

Jay sat down on a bottom bunk. He liked the cozy feeling of it. He didn't know why his mother assumed he would want to sleep on the top.

Suddenly they heard a car horn outside.

"They're here!" called Mrs. Koota.

"They're here!" Ellen echoed.

They're here, Jay thought unhappily to himself. He had wanted more time to get to know this place before he had to meet all these strangers, too.

The Ross family had a big station wagon and their suitcases were strapped to the roof. "You haven't changed at all," Mrs. Ross said as she hugged Jay's mother.

"You liar. You haven't either," Mrs. Koota answered.

Jay was embarrassed to see his mother laughing like a kid. The two fathers were shaking hands. Jay looked at the younger Rosses. Stacey had blond ponytails like a girl in his class in school. Mickey, standing next to her, looked the way Jay wished that he could look. He was tall, and his stomach was flat so his T-shirt was tucked in evenly inside his jeans.

Everyone was introduced to everyone else. Mr. and Mrs. Ross wanted to be called Aunt Vera and Uncle Phil. Jay thought that was silly. They weren't related so why should they pretend that they were?

"We already have an Uncle Phil," said Ellen.

"My brother's name is Phil, too," said Mr. Koota.

"I guess I'm the fake Uncle Phil then," said Mr. Ross. That made all the grown-ups laugh.

"You call us Aunt Claire and Uncle Dave," Jay's mother told Mickey and Stacey.

"We stopped for a few groceries," said Aunt Vera as they began unloading the station wagon.

"I was in such a rush to get here I didn't even think about food," said Mrs. Koota. "In New York you can buy just about anything at any hour."

"You won't be able to do that here," said the fake Uncle Phil.

"We could pick berries like Hansel and Gretel," suggested Stacey.

"We could eat roots and berries and fish that we caught," said Mickey. "How's that sound?" he asked Jay.

Jay looked at the sandwiches that his mother was preparing. Salami sandwiches weren't much of a supper, but he would take them over berries and roots any day.

"According to the instructions the owner left, there's a supermarket just fifteen miles from here," said Mrs. Koota. "We can stock up tomorrow morning."

"How far is fifteen miles?" asked Ellen.

"It's the same as 300 city blocks," said her father.

Jay winced. Once there had been a bus strike, and he had to walk twelve blocks to school every day for two weeks. Jay had been very happy when the strike was over.

"After supper can we watch TV?" asked Ellen.

"I guess you didn't notice," said her father. "This house doesn't have a television set. Twelve beds but no TV."

"And no bears," said Ellen. "It isn't fair."

2

· Bunk Mates ·

Their parents finally decided that the boys would take one of the downstairs bedrooms and the girls the other. Jay could tell that Ellen felt grown-up sharing a room with Stacey. Ellen and Stacey had been giggling since supper. They had made a sign reading, No Boys Can Come In, and hung it on their bedroom door.

Jay wished getting to know someone could be that easy for him. It made Jay feel like a baby to share a room with a boy who was four years older and wore striped pajamas that looked like the kind fathers wore. Jay's pajamas had little sailboats on them.

Mickey immediately climbed into one of the top bunks in their room.

"I'm going to sleep down here," said Jay, arranging himself on the bottom of the other bed.

"Oh, come on. Bottoms are for babies," said Mickey. "Even the girls are sleeping in the top beds in their room."

It was impossible for Jay to remain on the bottom bunk. He climbed up cautiously and looked down. He just knew he would fall out of bed during the night. He wondered if he would be killed or if he would just dislocate his spine or crush his skull.

Then Jay thought of a plan. He would tuck the covers around himself so tightly he wouldn't be able to roll out. It wasn't easy, but he managed to get each side of the blanket under the mattress. Now he would be safe.

All four parents made the rounds to say good night. Jay was glad his mother wasn't able to reach up and kiss him. He could imagine how babyish that would seem to a boy Mickey's age.

As soon as the lights were turned out, Jay began to feel thirsty. It must have been the salami he ate at supper. He tried breathing with his mouth open to cool off his tongue but that didn't work. It only made him more thirsty. There was no way he was going to climb down the ladder in the dark. He would just have to stay thirsty.

"Knock, knock," said Mickey.

"What?" asked Jay.

"No, no. You're supposed to say 'who's there?' And then when I tell you, you ask 'who.' Now say it."

"Knock, knock," said Jay.

"No, no. 'Who's there?'"

"It's me," said Mrs. Koota opening the door a crack. "Do you guys have enough blankets?"

"We're fine," said Mickey.

Jay wanted to ask for a glass of water, but the door was shut too quickly.

"Knock, knock," said Mickey.

"Who's there?" said Jay, remembering how the game went.

"Good," said Mickey.

"Good who?" asked Jay.

"No, I mean it's good that you remembered to ask 'who's there?' Now let's start over. Knock, knock."

"Who's there?" asked Jay. It was easier to talk to Mickey in the dark.

"Atch."

"Atch who?"

"Gesundheit." said Mickey.

"I didn't sneeze," said Jay, but just at that moment something tickled his nose, and he let out a real sneeze.

"Hey, that's swell," said Mickey. "I never knew anyone who could sneeze whenever he wanted."

In the dark, Jay blushed. Maybe he could practice sneezing so that Mickey wouldn't find out that it had been an accident.

"I can belch," said Mickey, and he made a couple of authentic ones.

"Do you think there are any bears around

here?" Jay asked.

"Naw," said Mickey. "Too bad, though. I'd love to go back to school and tell everyone I saw one."

"Yeah." It was a good thing he wasn't attached to a lie detector, thought Jay. Everything he said to Mickey was a lie. It was going to be a tough two weeks.

Jay tried to find a more comfortable position, but it was hard to move with the blanket tucked so tightly around him and he didn't want to risk falling out of bed. He lay still waiting to fall asleep. But he had slept so much during the drive to Vermont, he was not the least bit tired.

Jay heard a rustling sound behind the wall. "What's that?" he asked Mickey.

Mickey stirred, half-asleep. "Prob'ly a mouse inside the woodwork."

Jay felt goose bumps under his pajamas. Mice were okay in cartoons and stories, but real mice gave him the shivers. He hoped there weren't any holes in the wall.

A mosquito buzzed around his head. It sounded twice as big as the New York City mosquitoes. He held his pillow over his face to keep from being bitten. The mosquito sounded farther away. Maybe it was biting Mickey.

Jay could hear the adults talking upstairs. He couldn't make out any words, just a mumble of voices. After a while he heard a door shut and then another. The grown-ups were going to bed. Except for an occasional rustling in the walls, all was quiet. Everyone was asleep except the mouse and him, Jay thought.

Suddenly a light was shining in Jay's eyes, and someone was tugging at his blanket. He tried to push him away. Someone poked him in the shoulder and a voice said, "Come on. Wake up!" Then Jay remembered that he was in the house in the woods. The voice was Mickey's.

"What do you want?" Jay asked.

"I heard something. I think there's a bear outside. Let's check it out."

Jay lay back in his bed. There was no way he was going to go out into the dark looking for a bear. "There aren't any bears here. You said so yourself. Besides bears are dangerous.

Maybe you better call your father."

"And miss my chance of seeing a bear?" said Mickey. "No way. He pulled the covers off Jay. "Come on. Don't be a Yellow Blue Jay."

"Maybe it's just your imagination," said Jay, ignoring Mickey's insult. He *was* yellow. He knew that.

Mickey handed his flashlight to Jay. "You hold this," he said. "I'll take my baseball bat."

"Are you going to play ball with the bear?" asked Jay, trying to joke.

"Stupid," said Mickey. "This is my weapon. I'm going to hit him over the head."

Jay was worried. Suppose the bear came at them too fast for Mickey to hit it? Suppose Mickey missed, but the bear didn't?

Just then they both heard something hit the ground with a thud. Slowly Jay climbed down the ladder from his bed and followed Mickey up the stairs to the front door. It was locked.

Jay held the flashlight so it shone on the door. He wished he was safe in his bed again.

Mickey turned the latch and the door opened. "This is it!" he whispered.

Jay stood in the doorway. Outside it was very dark. Of course there were no streetlights. There were no streets. As Jay's eyes adjusted he could make out the shapes of the bushes around the house and the trees. What was hiding behind the bushes?

Mickey pulled Jay by the arm. "Come on, Yellow Blue Jay," he said.

As his bare foot touched the ground, Jay suddenly had an amazing thought. He had never been outdoors at night without an adult before. There was a sound in the bushes to the right of the house. Jay stood absolutely still. He couldn't have run even if Mickey let go of his arm.

"That's the bear." whispered Mickey. "Shine the light over there."

Shivering, Jay moved the flashlight to shine in that direction. The light bobbed up and down. His teeth chattered. What kind of teeth did a bear have? he wondered. Probably very sharp ones.

The flashlight shook in Jay's hands. At his side, Mickey stood holding the baseball bat with both hands, as if he was expecting the

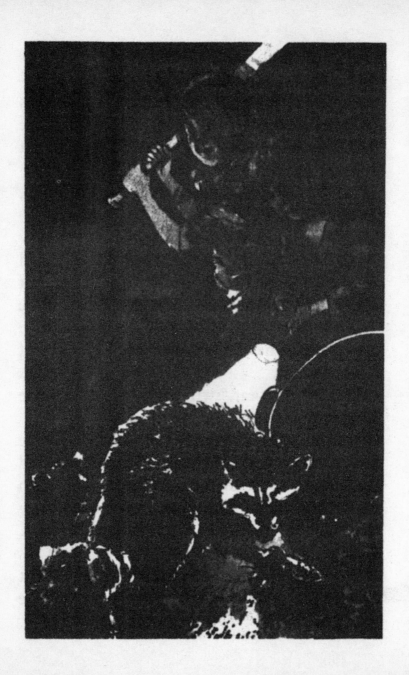

bear to pitch a ball his way. "Don't move the light so fast," Mickey said.

Jay turned the flashlight's beam to cover the bushes. Suddenly they saw something. Next to the overturned garbage can was an animal the size of a dog. Nearby were two smaller animals that were her babies. Jay had seen pictures of these animals at school. Instead of being frightened, he was so relieved he began laughing.

"That bear is a raccoon," he told Mickey.

Mickey lowered his bat. He and Jay stood watching as the raccoons finished their meal. The mother raccoon was chewing an old corncob. The animals did not seem at all bothered by the presence of the boys.

"They're having a better supper than we did," Jay said.

"That must be garbage from the people who were here before us," said Mickey.

Something tickled Jay's nose, and he gave two loud sneezes. The mother raccoon looked up, startled. She dropped her ear of corn and escaped into the bushes. Her babies followed.

"You scared her," said Mickey. "I wonder

if you could scare a bear with your sneezes."

Jay felt his nose begin to tickle again. It was too chilly to be standing barefoot outside. "Let's go in," he said to Mickey.

The two boys tiptoed back into the house and closed the door behind them. It felt good to get back into bed and under a warm blanket.

"Too bad it wasn't a bear," said Mickey.

"Yeah," Jay said yawning. Now that he was safe in bed he could almost agree.

Mickey yawned. "Tomorrow we can go exploring," he said. "I'm glad I've got you. Stacey's okay, but it's good to have another guy around."

Jay smiled in the dark. He was so tired he forgot to tuck himself in again. It didn't matter because in thirty seconds he was sound asleep.

3

· The First Morning ·
· in the Woods ·

When Jay woke up the next morning he was still in his top bunk. He hadn't fallen out of bed. Only thirteen more nights to go, he thought to himself. The bear hunt the night before seemed like a dream. Only his dirty feet were proof that it had really happened.

"How about making a few sneezes?" asked

Mickey as he pulled a clean T-shirt over his head.

"Not now," said Jay. "I have to be in the mood."

The boys went upstairs to get some breakfast, cold cereal and milk that Mrs. Ross had picked up the night before.

"It's not fair!" pouted Ellen as she ate her cornflakes. "You should have woke us up to see the raccoons."

Stacey nodded her head in agreement.

"I would have liked to photograph them," said Jay's father.

"They'll be back again," predicted Mrs. Koota. "Our instructions say the raccoons will get into the garbage every night unless we tie the pail shut."

"Well it's still not fair," complained Ellen.

"How would you girls like to help with the shopping this morning?" asked Aunt Vera. "Aunt Claire and I are driving into town, and you girls can come along."

Both girls seemed pleased with this invitation.

"Thank goodness we didn't have to go," said

Mickey. "Who wants to spend the morning in the supermarket?"

Jay agreed with Mickey. However, he did not feel comfortable about spending the time alone with the older boy. What would they do? What would they talk about?

The fathers were going for a drive in the other car. Jay wanted to go with them, but Mickey said, "We're going to explore the mountain." Jay thought of the explorers he had learned about in school: Columbus, Magellan, Vasco da Gama. What would he and Mickey find?

As the two boys started off, Jay realized his mother hadn't given him a single warning. In the city she always said things like, "Be careful crossing the street" and "Don't talk to strangers." Of course there were no streets here. There was not another car, house, nor person in sight. In the daylight, the thick bushes and tall trees seemed less frightening than they had the night before. Still, Jay was glad he wasn't alone.

The boys walked down the dirt road that led from the house. By the time they lost sight of their house it was almost as if they were the only people left in the world. Maybe this was what it was like for Columbus, Jay thought. Then he remembered that there had been Indians and the entire crew of the *Niña*, the *Pinta* and the *Santa Maria* hanging around. He and Mickey were all alone.

"Let's climb up the mountain." said Mickey. "It's not that far away."

Jay had once seen a movie about mountain climbers. They had ropes and picks to anchor themselves with, and it had been so scary that even sitting in his seat in the theater, he had felt dizzy.

"You need special boots to climb a mountain," said Jay. He tried to say it as if he had left his mountain climbing boots under his bed back home. But he knew he sounded unconvincing.

"This is a mountain for skiing. It won't be rocky. I think there is even a chair lift."

Jay didn't know what a chair lift was and didn't want to ask, so he just followed along behind Mickey. In the distance they could see a small house. Ellen would have probably insisted that it was the home of the Three Bears.

As they approached the house, Mickey pointed to a sign. "Look. The chair lift runs even during the summer."

The sign said that the lift ran hourly and that it cost one dollar and fifty cents for children and three dollars for adults.

"Rats!" said Mickey. "I don't have any money with me. Do you?"

"No," said Jay truthfully and happily. Now that they were there, he could see that the chair lift was a series of seats mounted on wires that went to the top of the mountain. It looked like a Ferris wheel, only it was a hundred times more frightening.

"I have an idea," said Mickey. He dashed off leaving Jay to wonder what he was up to.

A minute later, Mickey returned. "We're in luck. The guy who runs the lift says that if we climb the mountain, he'll give us a ride down for free."

Jay swallowed hard. The mountain was not nearly as steep as the one in the movie. Still, it was big. It was at least as big as one hundred city blocks.

"Suppose we only make it halfway up?" Jay asked.

"Then we'll have to turn around and walk back down," grinned Mickey. "But we can do it. It's not that tough. Come on," he urged. "Let's get started."

"Let's do it some other day," suggested Jay. "Now that we know where the mountain is, we can come here anytime."

"We always knew where the mountain was," said Mickey. "Come on."

Jay looked again and knew he wasn't going. "I have to go to the bathroom," he said. "Let's go back to the house."

"Go in the bushes," said Mickey.

"I can't," said Jay, turning beet red.

'Well. I'm going without you," said Mickey, and he turned away.

Jay stood watching Mickey as he climbed farther and farther up. Jay didn't really need the bathroom, but he didn't need to climb up the mountain either. And besides, he was already feeling hungry. You shouldn't have to climb a mountain with only a bowl of cornflakes inside you. The mountain climbers in the movie had eaten a big breakfast, and they carried chocolate bars with them for quick energy.

Jay turned back to the road that he and Mickey had taken. He might as well go back to the house. As he walked along, something tickled his nose and he sneezed. He tried to make himself sneeze again. How could he teach Mickey how to sneeze when he didn't know what made him do it in the first place?

Neither car was in the driveway. No one was home, and the door to the house was locked. Jay sat down on the doorstep, but after a couple of minutes he got up again.

There was not a sound: No car horns, no sirens, no radios, and no voices. But as Jay's ears became accustomed to the silence, he could hear the rustling of the leaves overhead, birds calling, and even the gurgle of the brook behind the house. Jay walked over to the brook. The sound it made reminded him of the water fountain at school. There was no path here, just trees and underbrush.

A pebble had gotten into Jay's sneaker, and he sat down on the ground to remove it. After he retied his sneaker, he remained sitting. Except for the brook and the buzz of an occasional insect, all was still. Jay breathed deeply, enjoying the smell of the damp earth and the pine trees around him. He could see nothing but trees and bushes. He wondered if anyone would be able to find him. He was so close to the house, and yet so perfectly hidden.

Jay picked up a small dead branch from the ground and broke it into smaller pieces. He stuck one of the pieces into the soft earth. Then he placed a second one nearby. He picked up a branch with pine needles stuck to it and balanced it on the top of the other two pieces. It began to look like a little house. On his hands and knees, Jay began to find other pieces of wood, dry bark that had fallen off trees, little pebbles, and bits of moss. He assembled these things and continued building. It was almost like working from one of his model kits except there was no glue and no instructions. The tiny house began to look cozy as Jay carpeted the inside with the velvety moss he found.

When he finished the first house, Jay built a second one leaning against a tree root. It was even more elaborate than the first with a tiny

path made of pebbles on two sides. As he worked, Jay wondered if Mickey would like to build little houses with him. Then he realized it was a silly idea. Mickey would think it was babyish. Mickey liked hunting bears and climbing mountains. He wouldn't want to do this.

Jay heard the sound of a car arriving. Then he heard voices. It was the girls and the mothers and the groceries. He wouldn't tell them what he had done either. It would be his secret. He wiped his hands on his jeans and stood up. Pine needles stuck to him and he brushed them off.

A second car arrived. The fathers were home now, too. Nobody noticed Jay as he made his way through the clearing and back to the driveway. The station wagon was filled with bags of groceries. It looked like enough to feed a hundred people for a year. Jay had forgotten how hungry he was, but now he remembered it again.

"Give us a hand," said Mrs. Koota.

Jay picked up one of the bags and started toward the house.

"Where's Mickey?" asked Aunt Vera.

"He's gone up the mountain," said Jay.

"The mountain? Isn't that dangerous?" asked Mrs. Koota.

"It's not dangerous," called out a voice. It was Mickey and he was grinning from ear to ear. "It was a piece of cake," he said.

"We bought a cake for supper," announced Stacey.

"Chocolate," said Ellen.

"Good," said Jay. But he wished they could have it for lunch.

4

· Snake Lake ·

"It's not fair," said Ellen as they gathered around the table for lunch. "Stacey and I didn't get to climb the mountain."

"The mountain won't go away," promised her mother. Then she turned to Jay. "Why didn't you go hiking with Mickey?" she asked.

Jay didn't say anything. He might try

climbing the mountain one of these days. But now, all he really cared about was getting some food into his stomach.

"I'm allergic to lettuce on sandwiches," Ellen told Aunt Vera. She always said she was allergic to something when she didn't want to eat it.

Jay bit down on his tuna sandwich with lettuce. It felt good to finally be eating some real food. It had been fun making the little houses, and he hoped he could sneak away and do it again after lunch. But a moment later his pleasure vanished.

"What shall we do this afternoon?" asked Uncle Phil.

"Let's go swimming in Snake Lake," said Jay's father. It doesn't look too far away on the map."

Snake Lake! The name sent chills down Jay's spine. He could hardly swallow. It was bad enough that he didn't know how to swim. He wasn't putting a foot into a lake filled with snakes.

I just won't go in the water, Jay told himself as everyone went to change into bathing suits. How could they all be so calm about Snake Lake?

When Jay pulled on his trunks, he remembered another reason why he never liked swimming. He hated the way his stomach rolled out over the top of his trunks. "You've got a spare tire," the salesman had said when he tried on the trunks in the store back home. Maybe when he was twelve he would have a flat stomach like Mickey. But that seemed very far away.

The Rosses and the Kootas all piled into the station wagon. Mr. Koota studied the map and gave directions.

Maybe we'll get lost, Jay thought. But that did not happen. In fifteen minutes the car drove up at Snake Lake.

There was no one in sight when they parked the car. "Our own private lake." sighed Mrs. Koota. "Do you know what Jones Beach looks like on a sunny day in August? Wall-to-wall people."

It's no wonder there were no other people, thought Jay. People in Vermont were too smart to go into a lake full of snakes.

"Where is the sand?" asked Ellen as they got

out of the car. There was grass growing right down to the water's edge.

"No sand. This isn't a beach," her father explained.

"It isn't fair," whined Mickey, imitating Ellen. Jay started laughing.

"Mickey!" said Uncle Phil.

"What did I do?" he asked innocently.

"Don't be a wise guy," said his father.

Mickey shrugged and stepped into the water. "It's not cold," he reported.

Jay watched as Mickey dove into the water. He didn't seem to be afraid of the snakes at all. Jay sat down on his towel and watched. Soon Mickey's head emerged from the water, and Jay could see he was headed toward a raft anchored farther out in the lake. It looked so easy watching. Jay knew that he would never be able to do that, not if he lived to be a hundred, even if there were no snakes to worry about. The girls were splashing each other. No one cared that they couldn't swim, he thought. But just then, Stacey jumped up and ran into the water. She could swim and she was only seven years old!

Jay's parents and Aunt Vera and Uncle Phil

sat on their towels talking. Grown-ups could think of things to talk about day and night.

"Look what I found!" Ellen suddenly shrieked. She was standing by the water's edge, looking at something. She must have found one of the snakes, Jay thought, shuddering.

Stacey swam back to see what Ellen had discovered.

"Come here," she called to Jay.

There was no way Jay wanted to go see a snake. But then he heard his father's voice, "Go and play with the others."

Reluctantly Jay got up and walked over to the girls.

"There are loads of them," called Ellen. "Hurry. Let's see how many we can catch."

The ground was covered with tiny frogs. They were jumping all over. Jay was relieved that they weren't snakes. But he didn't like frogs, either. Ellen had one in her hand, and when she tried to grab a second one, she lost the first.

"Aren't they cute?" asked Stacey. She held one out to Mickey who had just returned from his swim.

"Put the ones you get into this pail," said Mickey, holding up a red plastic bucket that someone had left near the water's edge.

"Here's one," said Ellen putting her frog inside the pail.

Ellen and Stacey and Mickey rushed around trying to catch the little frogs. Jay bent down and pretended he was trying, too. But he had no intention of touching one of those little creatures. They were ugly, and maybe they would bite or sting when you touched them.

Mickey caught a frog in each hand and put them into the pail. Then Stacey added one to the collection, and Ellen came up with another.

"What are you going to do with 'em all?" Jay asked.

"Some people eat frog's legs," said Mickey.

Jay felt his stomach lurch.

"Oh, Mickey. We couldn't eat these cute little frogs," laughed Stacey.

"I'm allergic to frogs," said Ellen.

"He's only teasing," said Stacey. "Besides, I don't think my mother knows how to cook frogs."

Jay let out his breath with relief. For a minute he had thought that eating frogs was a custom in Ohio. He squatted down beside the pail and looked at the little frogs splashing around inside.

"Don't let them escape," said Ellen.

"Don't worry," said Jay. He wondered if these little frogs were frightened. The frogs jumped on top of one another and one almost jumped out of the pail.

Jay didn't want to put his hands over the pail, so he looked around to see if there was another way of covering the top. He ran and got his towel.

"Having fun?" asked his mother. She was lying in the sun trying to get a tan.

"We're catching frogs," said Jay.

"That's something you've never done before," said Mrs. Koota. "There are no frogs for you to catch in New York."

Thank goodness for that, Jay thought as he ran back to the pail. He put the towel on top so that the frogs couldn't get out.

"Good thinking," said Mickey as he moved the towel aside and put in two more frogs. "Let's take a swimming break and come back to the frogs later," he said to Jay.

Jay took a deep breath. "I can't swim," he blurted out. Better to say it right away than to put it off. Swimming wasn't something you could pretend about like sneezing.

"It's easy. I'll teach you," offered Mickey. "Then later you can teach me your sneezing trick. It would drive my teachers crazy if I had sneezing fits in class. You can't scold a kid for sneezing."

Jay walked reluctantly toward the water. He would rather catch frogs than go swimming in Snake Lake.

"You have to get in fast," said Mickey. "Then it doesn't feel cold."

Jay shivered as Mickey splashed water at him.

"Look," said Mickey. "You can practice floating right here at the edge." He lay down in the shallow water and bobbed up and down. "See. I couldn't drown if I wanted to."

Jay knew he was much fatter than Mickey. He was sure he would sink. But he let himself lay down and be supported by the older boy. "Don't let go," he pleaded. Mickey removed first one hand then the other. "See. You're floating," he announced.

Jay put his foot down to feel the pebbly bottom of the lake.

"Help," he sputtered.

Mickey helped him stand up. "Come on. Don't be a baby, Yellow Blue Jay. You were doing it for a second."

Jay remembered how Mickey had called him that the night before. It made him angry. He wouldn't be yellow. He'd show Mickey. He lay back in the water again.

"Relax," said Mickey. "You can do it."

Jay took a deep breath and tried not to think of a snake swimming underneath him. Suddenly Jay thought of something that he had learned in school. Snakes were reptiles. That meant they couldn't breathe in the water. If there were any snakes around, they would have to be on land. He was probably safer in the water. Jay relaxed.

"That's good," said Mickey. "That's the way."

It wasn't swimming, but it was a beginning.

Jay stayed in the water a long time. Mickey was a better teacher than the swimming counselor at day camp. Or maybe it was just easier to learn when there weren't so many kids jumping around and splashing, as there was at camp.

"You'll see. By the time you go home, you'll be swimming," Mickey promised Jay.

"Kids," called Aunt Vera. "It's getting cloudy. I think we may have some rain."

Jay blinked the water from his eyes. The sky was darker than it had been a little while ago.

"Can we take the frogs back to the house with us?" Ellen asked her parents.

"Better not," Mrs. Koota called back. "You don't want to separate them from all their relatives."

There was one huge load of frogs in the pail.

"Let's count them," said Stacey.

Mickey stuck his hand in the pail and gently removed a handful of frogs. "One, two three . . ." he counted as he released them. The frogs began hopping in all directions.

"Four, five, six . . ."

"Hurry kids," called Uncle Phil.

"Seven, eight, nine . . ."

"Too bad we can't take some back with us," said Ellen. "We could leave them in the bathtubs."

"But how could we take a shower?" asked Stacey. "We might step on them."

"Ten, eleven, twelve . . ."

Jay felt something brush against his foot. He looked down and saw one of the little frogs.

"Thirteen, fourteen, fifteen . . ."

If he was brave enough to float, thought Jay, then he was brave enough to pick up a frog. He watched the tiny body inflate and deflate as it breathed inside his hand. It didn't feel the least bit prickly or clammy.

"Sixteen, seventeen, eighteen . . ."

"Don't be afraid,'" Jay whispered to the little creature in his hand. "I won't hurt you." Gently, he placed the frog back down on the ground. He wasn't a Yellow Blue Jay.

"Nineteen, twenty, twenty-one . . ."

There was a gust of wind and a clap of thunder in the distance.

"Okay. Let's get going," called Jay's father.

"Twenty-two. Twenty-two frogs," shouted

Mickey as he let the last one go free.

The four children ran toward the car and were safely inside before the first drops of rain began to fall.

Jay sat between Mickey and Ellen in the backseat. He looked at his hands. He had held a frog. And he had floated, too. What a day this had been!

"What's for supper?" asked Mickey.

"Hamburgers." called out Mrs. Koota above the sound of the rain drumming on the roof of the car.

"We could have had frogburgers," Mickey said.

"Ooooh, that's mean," said Ellen.

"You're allergic to frogs," Stacey reminded her.

Before long they were back in the house, snug against the storm outside. The hamburgers tasted much better than hamburgers did at home.

Before he went to sleep that night, Jay studied the map of Vermont. He found the mountain Mickey had climbed and he found the lake.

"Hey," he called out. "I just figured out why they call it Snake Lake. It's the shape. It's long and skinny and it twists around."

"That's not fair," said Ellen. "They should call it Frog Lake. I never saw so many frogs before in my life."

"I don't think you ever saw *any* frogs before in your life," said her mother.

Jay smiled to himself. Too bad he hadn't known about the lake's name before they had gone swimming. It would have saved him a lot of worrying. He hoped the rain would be finished by tomorrow. He was eager to get back into the water and practice his swimming.

· 5 ·

· The Kids ·
· on Kitchen Patrol ·

The days began to follow a pattern. The next morning they all piled into the station wagon and drove north to see some little towns with quaint houses and quaint shops. It wasn't very exciting, thought Jay, but he preferred it to mountain climbing. The following morning it was raining. Jay was glad nature had given him another excuse not to climb the mountain. By the afternoon, the weather turned bright and warm and they had returned to Snake Lake. Now that he knew there were no snakes, Jay looked forward to practicing his swimming. He felt more confident every day. Maybe he could be in the Minnow swimming group at day camp next summer. It was almost possible that he would be ready for the Salmons.

It wasn't often that Jay had any time by himself. But when he could, he would disappear into the woods. He liked the quiet that wasn't really quiet at all. He could hear insects buzzing and birds chirping overhead. Even the leaves made a special sound as they moved with the breezes. With the sun poking through the treetops and lighting little spots all around him, Jay felt safe and cozy. But best of all he liked taking the little branches, the pieces of bark, and the bits of moss that he found and forming tiny houses. By the end of the first week in the woods, he had made a dozen. They were so cleverly hidden that he didn't think anyone would ever see them.

Once or twice, lying in his bunk at night,

Jay almost told Mickey about the houses. But each time, he stopped and said nothing. A twelve-year-old boy was sure to think that building little houses in the woods was a baby game.

In the evening, there was no television to watch. Sitting around in the living room with another family was like having company all the time. Aunt Vera always knit after supper. She was making a sweater for Stacey. First the back and then the front of the sweater grew from the long knitting needles. Now she was working on one of the sleeves.

Mrs. Koota and the fathers read and talked at the same time. That would never have been allowed at school!

Mickey and Jay and Stacey and Ellen spent the evenings playing board games that the Rosses had brought from Ohio.

Aunt Vera and Jay's mother took turns preparing dinner. One night they had chicken, another night there was spaghetti. When Aunt Vera made the sauce for the spaghetti there were big lumps of tomatoes and onions in it, not smooth the way it was when Mrs. Koota made it. Jay thought it tasted pretty good, but Ellen said, "I'm allergic to this spaghetti."

One day Aunt Vera made a pie using red celery. Jay had never heard of celery pie, but he tried it anyhow. It was delicious, and he wished there was enough for seconds.

"I'm allergic to celery," Ellen complained when the pie was being served.

"This isn't celery. It's rhubarb," Aunt Vera said. But then Ellen complained that she was also allergic to rhubarb.

One evening as they were finishing supper, Mrs. Koota said, "I think the mothers deserve a holiday, too. How about you men making dinner tomorrow evening?"

"I've got a better idea," said Mr. Koota. "Why don't we go to a restaurant?"

"It's too expensive for eight people to eat out," said Aunt Vera. "Phil, won't you and Dave give it a try?"

"It's only fair," said Ellen.

So the next evening, the fathers prepared supper. They made everyone leave the house, so when Jay and Ellen and Mickey and Stacey and their mothers returned from Snake

Lake they were all expecting a big surprise. The surprise was that they were having hamburgers again for the second night in a row, and two of the baked potatoes burst inside the oven.

"Dynamite!" said Mickey as the first potato exploded.

"You're supposed to prick the potatoes with a fork before you put them in to bake," Mrs. Ross said. "You'll know next time."

"You mean there is going to be a next time?" asked Uncle Phil. "I thought this got us off the hook."

"How about letting us make dinner tomorrow night?" Jay suggested.

"Us?" said his mother. "Us who?"

"Us kids," said Jay, looking to Mickey for support.

"Yes. Yes," agreed Stacey. "We made applesauce at school."

"We made popcorn," said Ellen.

"Popcorn and applesauce? What kind of meal is that?" asked Mickey. "Forget it."

"I think it's a great idea," said Mrs. Koota.

Everyone, thought it was a great idea—except Mickey. Jay was sorry that he had said anything. It wasn't like him to come up with a plan like this. And now, if Mickey wasn't going to help, he didn't want to be involved.

"Okay, it's settled then," said Aunt Vera. "Tomorrow we'll take you kids to town to buy whatever supplies you need. And you can use anything that is already in the house."

"Great," said Mickey sarcastically as the four kids sat together on the floor in the boys' bedroom to discuss their cooking strategy. "Not only do we have to make dinner tomorrow, we're going to lose a whole morning grocery shopping. I wanted to go mountain climbing."

"We'll go the day after tomorrow," Jay promised, before he could think better of it.

"Grocery shopping isn't so bad," said Stacey. "Ellen and I like going shopping."

"Well, I don't," said Mickey crossly. "And besides," he said looking at Jay. "What do you know how to cook?"

"Nothing," Jay admitted. "But we could find a recipe in a cookbook."

"Okay wise guy," said Mickey. "How many cookbooks did you happen to bring on vacation with you?"

Jay hadn't thought of that. At home his

mother had loads of cookbooks. "I know," he said after a minute. "Did you ever look in those magazines our mothers buy in the supermarket? They have recipes in them."

"I know where one is right now," shouted Ellen and she dashed out of the room. She returned with a magazine.

"There's got to be something in here," said Jay as he began to turn the pages. He flipped past fashions for the fall season and stopped when he came to TEN NEW WAYS TO COOK HAMBURGER.

"Not hamburger again," moaned Stacey.

Jay kept turning. "Look at this!" he exclaimed.

"Shish kabob," read Ellen, sounding out the word.

"I had that once in a restaurant," said Mickey. "It's good," he admitted.

Jay began reading the recipe. "It says you can use lamb or beef," he reported. "I've seen my mother buy packages with the meat all cut into pieces like this when she is going to make a stew. So that part is easy." He looked at Mickey. "I told you we could do it."

He looked back at the recipe. "Tomatoes, green peppers, onions, and mushrooms," he read as he admired the full-page picture in the magazine. It showed the pieces of meat and the vegetables strung together on metal rods.

"Just one problem," said Mickey. He pointed to the rods. "These are called skewers," he said. "Where are you gong to get them?"

"Couldn't we just get some sticks in the woods?" asked Ellen.

"They'd catch fire while the meat was cooking," said Mickey.

"We don't have to put them on the skewers," suggested Stacey.

"The whole point of shish kabob is the skewers," said Mickey. "Remember, I'm the only one here who ever ate it. No skewers, no shish kabob." He pointed to the magazine. "Keep turning," he said to Jay.

"No," said Jay. "I'll find some skewers, and we'll make shish kabob."

"Where will you get them?" asked Ellen.

"I don't know yet," said Jay. "But I'll figure out something."

In the morning, their mothers drove them

to the supermarket. They presented Mickey with a twenty-dollar bill. "This should cover everything," said Mrs. Koota. "But we'll be waiting outside in case you need money or advice."

"We may need more money, but we won't need any advice," said Jay. He felt in charge of this venture. After all, it had been his idea. If only he could find skewers in the supermarket.

Stacey pushed the shopping wagon and Mickey and Jay put the food inside. They bought all the things the recipe called for. The magazine suggested serving shish kabob over rice, so they bought a two-pound box.

"You need lemons," Ellen reminded her brother. So Stacey steered the cart back toward the produce aisle. Before it was put on the skewers, the meat had to soak in lemon juice and spices. The spices were all things like ginger, garlic, and ground red pepper; when they had checked in the kitchen, everything was there. Only the skewers were still missing.

There was an aisle of kitchen supplies. Jay saw serving forks and wooden spoons, potholders and dish towels. He did not see any skewers.

"There aren't any here," said Mickey, who had been watching Jay. "So what are you going to use?"

Jay just shrugged. "You'll see this afternoon," he promised.

A mother with three little girls was on line in front of them. "Brooke, Fern, Willow," she scolded them. They were eating cookies from a box that hadn't been paid for yet.

Jay thought they had country names. He tried to imagine some city names: Sewer, Traffic, Hydrant. Then the girls and the cookies reminded him that they hadn't planned any dessert.

"Do we have enough money for ice cream?" he asked Mickey.

Mickey began mentally totaling their purchases and nodded his head.

"Let's get vanilla, and Ellen and I will pick some blackberries to put on top of it," said Stacey.

Ellen and Stacey ran off to the freezer section and came back with the ice cream. Soon everything was paid for.

"What do you have in those bags?" asked Mrs. Koota.

None of the children would give her even a little hint.

After the lunch dishes had been cleared away, the children put the meat to marinate. That meant it had to soak in the lemon juice and spices before cooking. Then Stacey and Ellen went off to pick berries. Jay searched the house for a substitute for the skewers. He examined the curtain rods in his bedroom. They were too thick.

"Boys, we're going to pick berries, too," said Aunt Vera. "You're on your own."

"No problem," said Mickey.

Because the stove was electric and didn't involve lighting matches, the parents had agreed to stay out of the kitchen. "Shout if there's a problem," said Mrs. Koota. "We won't be very far off."

The boys nodded.

Back in the kitchen, Jay and Mickey cut up the vegetables.

"Quit stalling," said Mickey. "Do you have skewers or don't you?"

"Let me think," Jay said. There must be

something in the house that he could use. Then he noticed Aunt Vera's knitting bag on a chair. "I've got them," he shouted.

Mickey looked puzzled. "Where are they?"

Jay opened Aunt Vera's knitting bag, and took out a pair of needles. He slid the metal needles out of the knitting. There was another pair of needles in the bag and he took those, too. "This should do just fine," said Jay.

"My mother will kill you," laughed Mickey. "How did you ever think of them?"

"Cooking is a snap," said Jay as he emptied the box of rice into a pot. He decided to use all of it. Two pounds of rice didn't look like nearly enough for eight people. "I don't know why our mothers complain about cooking."

"It must get boring," pointed out Mickey. "They have to do it over and over day after day."

"Eating doesn't get boring," said Jay. "We always want to eat."

"Not when it's hamburgers three nights in a row," said Mickey. "But this meal is going to be super."

Jay beamed as he threaded the meat and

vegetables onto the metal rods.

Mrs. Ross' knitting needles were the perfect skewers for shish kabob! The platter with the meat and vegetables looked just as good as it did in the magazine photograph. Mr. Koota ran to get his camera to record the meal.

"You've never taken pictures of my meals," Mrs. Koota complained. But she wasn't really annoyed.

Mrs. Ross was surprised when she recognized her knitting needles on the serving platter.

"You said we could use anything in the house," Jay pointed out.

"I meant pots and pans and spices—things in the kitchen," laughed Aunt Vera.

"Sometimes you knit in the kitchen," said Stacey.

"Not only are they good cooks, they are good lawyers, too," said Uncle Phil.

There was enough rice for all of them and enough for the next two nights as well.

"Rice expands when it cooks," Jay's mother explained.

"At least it doesn't explode," said Mickey.

"This is one of the best meals I've ever eaten," admitted Aunt Vera. She helped herself to a second portion. Even Ellen forgot that she was allergic to green peppers and enjoyed the meal.

"It's really Jay who should get all the credit," said Stacey. "It was his idea."

"Jay, I'm going to make you a sweater," said Aunt Vera. "I want you to see what knitting needles are really meant for."

· 6 ·

· Mountain Climbers ·

There was no way that he could get out of it. Jay had promised he would climb the mountain with Mickey. It wasn't raining. There was no trip planned. The mountain and Mickey were waiting and Jay had to go.

"We can't go," said Stacey. "We're going to make jam."

Making jam out of the wild blackberries had been Mrs. Koota's idea. "Imagine eating jam on some cold morning in January that was made from berries we picked in Vermont in August," she said.

Jay wished it was January now and he didn't have to go up the mountain. But it wasn't and he did.

After a breakfast of pancakes with Vermont maple syrup, the two boys started off. "I can't wait to get home and tell people I climbed a mountain," said Mickey. "Ohio is very flat."

Jay knew that on the first day of school his fourth-grade teacher would ask everyone to write a report on what they had done during the summer. "How I Climbed a Mountain" by Jay Koota sounded pretty good. On the other hand, he would just as soon write a report called "How My Friend Mickey Climbed a Mountain." Everyone would be impressed that he had a twelve-year-old friend who did things like that. "Wait up," he called to Mickey now. "Your legs are longer than mine."

Mickey slowed down. "Sorry," he said.

Mickey was a really a nice guy. Jay knew

he didn't have to wait up for a short, fat kid. He wished the kids at school who made fun of his weight and his name, calling him "Cootie Head," could see him walking down the road with Mickey Ross.

"Too bad there's no snow on top of the mountain," said Mickey. "You know, like those pictures in the geography books at school."

"Yeah," Jay agreed. "We have those same books in New York."

As they began to climb the mountain Mickey pointed to a small sign that read, BEGINNER'S LUCK. "This must be the ski trail for beginners. You'll see, it's an easy climb."

"Yeah. But the skiers go down and we're going up," said Jay. His knees ached, and he was out of breath. He was also thirsty. Maple syrup always left him thirsty.

"Turn around and look down," said Mickey. Jay did and was pleased to see how far they had come already.

"Of course when I tell them about it at school," said Mickey, "I won't let on it was so easy."

"Right," panted Jay.

The two boys continued up the mountain. Jay felt more and more thirsty. Real mountain climbers carried canteens of water. They also carried chocolate bars for energy. What he would really like was a chocolate ice-cream soda or maybe a chocolate malted. He stopped to catch his breath. Mickey never needed to stop at all.

"Hey, look. The chair lift is coming up," Mickey called to him.

Jay watched as the chairs swung by on the wire cord overhead. A voice boomed out. "Good work, Sir Hillary! Keep it up!"

Jay saw a man with a big moustache and a bright green shirt passing by in one of the chairs. Behind him sat a woman who also waved, and in the next chair behind her sat two teenage girls huddled close together.

"Who's Sir Hillary?" asked Jay as the chairs moved up the mountain ahead of them.

"He's the man who climbed Mount Everest," said Mickey. "It's just about the highest mountain in the world. That's one of the questions when you play Trivial Pursuit."

Jay felt as if he was climbing the highest

mountain in the world himself. He tried to concentrate on some part of his body that didn't hurt. His pinky on his right hand felt fine. So as he continued to climb behind Mickey, he kept thinking about his little finger. He began to feel a tingling sensation in his right hand. He looked at his pinky. There was nothing to see. Hands don't get hungry and tired when you are using your feet.

"Turn around and look down now," called Mickey who was quite far ahead.

Jay turned and nearly lost his balance. He was so high up that he really felt dizzy. It reminded him of the time his parents took him and Ellen to the World Trade Center in New York.

"We're almost at the top. Look at that sign," said Mickey, pointing to a trail marker that said, THE JAWS OF DEATH.

Perfect, thought Jay. It was just the way he felt. He couldn't remember ever being so hot and tired. He just wanted to lie down somewhere. But he put one foot in front of the other and continued up the mountain.

The man in the green shirt and his family

were waiting to greet the boys when they reached the top. "Congratulations!" he called to them. "That's quite a hike."

"It's easy. This was the second time I've done it," said Mickey.

It wasn't easy, Jay thought. But I've done it. I really did do it. I've climbed a mountain. He stood looking down and marveled that he had made it to this height. He felt as if he was king of the world standing there so high and looking down at the tiny people who were getting on the chair lift below. Suddenly he no longer felt tired. He felt terrific.

The man in the green shirt was already climbing back into the chair lift for his return trip down the mountain. But Jay was in no hurry to leave. "Maybe the next time we come, my father will let me take his camera," he said to Mickey. Five minutes at the top had changed his whole feeling about mountain climbing. He was already planning to do it again.

"We better get going," said Mickey. "It's almost lunchtime."

Jay was so excited he had even forgotten to be hungry. It wasn't often that the alarm clock in his stomach forgot to remind him about eating. Now, looking at the chair lift, he lost his appetite. High wasn't his top bunk bed. High was sitting in the chair lift on the top of the mountain.

"Are we going to sit together?" he asked.

"It's more fun if we each have our own seat," said Mickey, climbing into the chair behind Jay.

Jay noticed that there was a small strap across each seat. Maybe it would keep you from falling out of the chair. But what happened if the wires that supported the chairs broke? What good was that little strap then?

The motor was switched on and the lift began to move. Jay felt sick. It would be terrible if he vomited all the way down the mountain. Quickly he closed his eyes and tried to think about something else. He moved his toes inside his sneakers and tried to think about them. He opened his eyes for a second and shut them again fast. It was a good thing he wasn't sitting next to Mickey, after all. He didn't want Mickey to know he was a Yellow Blue Jay for sure.

Jay opened his eyes again. They were already halfway down; the wires had proven their strength. This is fun, Jay realized suddenly. He felt almost as if he were in a swing in the playground, except that he didn't have to pump his legs to keep moving. It was as if he were a bird, so high above everything. He turned around to look at Mickey.

"This is neat," he called to him.

"We can do it again tomorrow," Mickey called back.

"I climbed the mountain," Jay announced proudly when he got back to the house.

"That's nice, dear," said Mrs. Koota, looking up. "We made a dozen jars of jam and we have enough berries for a pie, too."

"Good," said Jay. He had never had a blackberry pie before, but he was sure he would like it. He had never met a pie he didn't like.

· 7 ·

· Bat Man ·

Lying in bed that night, Jay had trouble falling asleep. He listened to the mouse moving around inside the wall. The sound was no longer frightening. It was just part of the night in Vermont. Jay had never seen the mouse, but one evening it ran across the living room floor. Jay's mother screamed so loudly that every-

one jumped, and Aunt Vera began scream-
ing, too.

That night Jay's mosquito bites itched worse
than ever. He and Mickey were having a con-
test. They wanted to see who would get the
most bites. Jay was winning. In one week, he
had gotten nineteen mosquito bites. That was
more than he had gotten during the entire
month of July and half of August at home. Jay
knew that many of those bites came during the
times he spent in the woods working on his
little houses. He tossed and turned thinking he
would never fall asleep. Then, just as he was
dozing off, there was a shout from upstairs.

Jay jolted awake. "I bet the mouse has come
back," he called to Mickey. They both ran
upstairs to investigate.

"Your mother really goes bonkers when she
sees a mouse," Mickey said.

In the living room, standing with her hands
over her head, was Aunt Vera. "It's a bat!"
she shrieked. "It just flew in the window." A
black thing was hanging from the curtain."

"Stay calm," said Uncle Phil. "It won't
hurt you."

"Maybe it's a vampire bat," suggested Jay.

"Sometimes bats are rabid," said Mickey.

"Is it still there?" called Jay's mother. She came out of her bedroom wearing a kerchief on her head.

Seeing her, Aunt Vera rushed to her room to get a scarf for her head.

Awakened by the noise, Stacey and Ellen had come upstairs, too.

"Ooooh. It's so ugly," said Ellen.

Jay thought it looked like something out of a science-fiction movie.

Uncle Phil took the dish towel from the kitchen and flipped it toward the bat. "If we open the door he might fly out," he suggested.

"Or the rest of his family might fly in," said Mrs. Koota.

"Aren't bats blind?" asked Mickey. "How can he see if the door is open or closed?"

The flipping of the towel startled the bat. It left its hold on the curtain and began to circle the room. Jay's mother let out another shriek, and Aunt Vera and the girls began shouting, too.

The bat swooped in the direction of Aunt

Vera. "Help!" she screamed and raced toward her bedroom. "I'm not coming out until you catch that thing," she called from behind the closed door. "I don't care if I spend the rest of the summer here." Mrs. Koota felt the same way and joined her in the bedroom.

"This is fun!" laughed Ellen. "It's almost as good as a bear."

"I think I'll write a report on it for school," said Mickey. "I'll call it 'The Night the Bat Got In.' "

"Fine. But how will it end?" asked his father.

The bat seemed tired now. It circled more slowly as if looking for a place to land.

"It's stopping," said Stacey as the bat took hold of one of the curtains again. This time, however, it was higher than before—out of the reach of Uncle Phil's towel.

"I've got an idea," said Mickey. He ran downstairs and came back with his baseball bat. "I'm going to bat the bat with my bat," he said swinging it.

"Hold it," said Mr. Koota. "I'm responsible for returning this house to the owners in one piece."

Jay's eyes landed on the garbage pail in front of the sink. He removed the plastic bag that was inside with the remains from their supper. He had an idea!

"What are you going to do?" asked Mr. Koota.

"*Shhh*," whispered Jay.

"If you catch the bat in that pail, he'll just fly out again," said Uncle Phil.

Jay pushed a chair toward the window and climbed up on it. Now he was just the right height. "Get a newspaper," he whispered to Mickey.

"You guys don't have to whisper. I don't think bats understand English," said Uncle Phil, but he was whispering, too. He ran into his bedroom to get the newspaper that lay on the floor.

"Did you catch it yet?" asked Aunt Vera.

"No," he said rushing back to the living room.

"I'm taller. Let me do it," said Mickey.

Jay shook his head. It was his idea. "Give me the paper," he said.

Uncle Phil handed it up to him.

Carefully Jay lifted the garbage pail and covered the bat and the part of the curtain it clung to. The bat let go of the curtain, and Jay could feel it hitting the sides of the pail trying to get free. With one hand, he held the pail and with the other, Jay slid the newspaper over the top of it. He climbed down from the chair flushed with success. "Here is the bat," he said. It was the best thing he had ever done.

"Great work!" Jay's father congratulated him.

"That was clever thinking," said Uncle Phil.

Ellen and Stacey skipped into the upstairs bedrooms. "Jay caught the bat. Jay caught the bat!" they shouted.

"Is it safe to come out?" asked Aunt Vera.

Mrs. Koota and Mrs. Ross returned to the living room. One wore a kerchief and the other a rain hat.

"Where is the bat now?" asked Mrs. Koota anxiously.

"In here," said Jay, pointing to the garbage pail. The newspaper covered the top so you couldn't see the bat. It had stopped fluttering inside the pail.

"You were very brave," said Jay's mother.

"If we just leave it inside the pail, it will suffocate," said Uncle Phil.

"Oh, no," squealed Ellen and Stacey.

"Can't we just let it go?" said Jay. "If we close the window, it won't come in again. It belongs out in the woods."

Mr. Koota closed the living room window. "We'll have to be careful not to open any windows that don't have screens," he said.

They opened the front door, and Jay carried the garbage pail outside. Standing back, so it wouldn't touch him, he slid the newspaper off the pail. For a moment, nothing happened, and then suddenly into the darkness there fluttered something even darker than the night. The bat was free.

Everyone returned to the house. "What a night!" said Aunt Vera as she removed her rain hat.

"First the raccoons, then a mouse, and now a bat," laughed Mrs. Koota. "What next?"

"How about a bear?" asked Ellen.

"No bears," said Mr. Koota firmly. "You can't catch bears with a garbage pail and a newspaper."

"Don't forget the frogs," Stacey remembered. "We caught them with a pail."

"Nice work, Jay," said Mickey. "You were great!"

"We'll have to call you Bat Man," said Uncle Phil, slapping Jay on the back.

"Yeah," said Mickey. "You can write a report for school: 'The bat strikes at midnight.'"

Jay looked at the kitchen clock. It was only ten-twenty. Still the title sounded good, and it made him feel good, too. No one could call him yellow *now*. He went back to bed feeling so happy that even his itchy mosquito bites couldn't bother him.

8

· Roger ·

The house in the woods had a telephone with a party line. That meant if the phone rang once and paused and then rang again, they were not supposed to answer it. The call was for someone at another house in the woods. But, if there were two rings, a pause, and two more rings, then the call was for them.

For the first few days, they had all looked at the phone whenever it rang. But it was never for them. Then one day, the telephone had rung twice, paused, and rung twice again. Mr. Koota grabbed it. Who could be calling them here?

It was a wrong number. After Mr. Koota hung up, Mrs. Ross said, "You know, I did give this number to friends who said they might be traveling around here. They probably won't come, but I invited them to drop by."

"Fine," said Mrs. Koota. "We have plenty of room."

Soon they all began to ignore the telephone. Even when it rang, it wasn't for them.

Then one evening as they were finishing dinner, Aunt Vera got a telephone call. "You must come," she said. "Come for lunch tomorrow. I can't wait to show you this house." She gave directions for the best route to take and how to locate the house in the woods. Finally, she hung up.

"That was Gloria Horak," she told everyone. "The Horaks live across the street from us."

"You mean Roger is coming here!" shouted Mickey. "Fantastic!"

"Roger is in Mickey's class at school," Aunt Vera explained to the Kootas. "The boys are great friends."

"We'll have a neat time," said Mickey.

Jay felt uneasy. Maybe Roger wouldn't want to spend time with an eight-year-old kid.

In the morning, the grown-ups rushed around setting the house in order.

"Put this puzzle away," Mrs. Koota told Jay.

"We're still in the middle of working on it," he complained.

"It takes up too much room," said his mother. "We'll be putting an extra leaf in the table at lunchtime."

At eleven-thirty, a car with Ohio plates drove up. "They're here! They're here!" shouted Mickey.

Why couldn't this Roger have stayed in Ohio? sighed Jay. Mickey would be going home in a few days and then he could be with Roger all the time.

Jay watched as the Horak family got out of their car. Seeing Roger standing next to Mickey made Jay suddenly feel smaller and younger than he had during the vacation here. He had almost forgotten there was a four-year difference in his and Mickey's ages. Mickey had treated him as an equal. Jay knew he wasn't twelve, but he hadn't felt like a little kid of eight, either. Now he did.

"Wait till you see where I sleep," said Mickey grabbing Roger's arm. "This house is loaded with bunk beds!"

The two older boys raced downstairs to the bedroom. Jay followed slowly behind. By the time he reached the bedroom, Mickey was sitting up in his bunk and Roger was sitting on Jay's bed. Jay wanted to tell him to get down, but he didn't. Instead he sat down on the floor and pretended that everything was just fine.

"This is Jay Koota," said Mickey, remembering that he hadn't introduced Roger to his bunk mate.

Roger laughed. "Cootie head. Jay Cootie Head. What a name!"

Jay blushed. Lots of kids called him that at school, and he had never gotten used to it.

"Boys!" came a shout from Aunt Vera.

Jay stood up, glad of a chance to escape from the room.

"Come on," Mickey said to Roger. "My mother's calling. It must be time for lunch."

The three families sat around the extended table to eat. "I'm going to buy some of this Vermont cheese to take home with us," said Mrs. Horak. Jay nibbled on a piece of cheese. Yesterday he had liked the cheese, too. Now with Roger sitting across the table next to Mickey, nothing tasted good anymore.

He looked at Ellen and Stacey, giggling together as usual. It didn't matter to them that the Horaks had come from Ohio. Lately they had a big secret that they wouldn't share with anyone. Jay didn't even care what the secret was.

As soon as lunch was over, Mickey suggested that Roger climb the mountain with him and Jay. "We've done it twice already," he said.

"You mean you do things with little Cootie Head here?" asked Roger, glancing in Jay's direction. "It's a good thing I showed up or you'd only have babies to play with."

Mickey shrugged his shoulders. "Jay's not so bad," he said.

"Well, does he have to come with us now?"
Mickey shrugged again. He seemed uncomfortable. Jay knew that he had just as much right to go up the mountain as anyone, but he didn't want to go with Roger.

"I don't want to go," he said.

"Are you sure?" asked Mickey, sounding relieved.

"Yeah," said Jay, trying to swallow the lump in his throat.

Jay watched as Mickey and Roger went off down the road to the mountain. Inside, the adults were still sitting around the table talking. Mrs. Koota was pouring out refills of coffee. The girls were probably in their bedroom coloring. This was the perfect time to go and check out his little houses, Jay thought.

As he made his way through the underbrush, Jay congratulated himself on having kept his secret. How many times had he wanted to share it with Mickey? He was glad Mickey didn't know about the little houses. He would certainly laugh about them with Roger. Mickey wasn't his friend, after all. Jay sniffed back a tear. He hated Roger Horak, and he hated Mickey Ross, too.

Jay had enjoyed the time he had spent constructing the houses almost as much as learning to swim at Snake Lake and climbing the mountain with Mickey. Now, as he looked at the first house he came to, it did not fill him with the pride that it usually did. What was he looking at? Just a few little twigs leaning against each other. It was silly. It was a babyish thing. Disgusted he kicked the little house. The twigs and moss scattered. Where a house had been standing a moment before, there was now nothing. The house was gone.

Suddenly Jay felt like destroying all the houses. He had hidden them well, but he knew where to look. First one and then another and another collapsed as he trampled on them. Stupid, stupid houses, he thought. The more he destroyed the more he wanted to destroy. He felt like a giant in one of the folk tales his mother had read to him when he was little. He liked the crunch as his sneakers landed on the twigs and each little house disappeared. In this little world that he had created, he was strong and powerful.

By the time he had crushed the last of the houses, Jay was exhausted. His T-shirt was

sticking to his back with sweat. It wasn't such hard work, not like climbing a mountain, but somehow it had worn him out. He sat down under one of the trees and leaned back, out of breath. He felt his heart beating. A mosquito buzzed by his ear. Jay felt too tired to even swat at it. What was another mosquito bite? He thought he heard Ellen and Stacey in the distance. They were probably looking for more berries. Slowly, his breathing returned to normal. He closed his eyes.

Jay turned his head and wondered why his pillow felt so hard. He opened his eyes and saw that he was not in his bed. He had fallen asleep in the woods. He didn't know what time it was. Stiffly he got up. He brushed the pine needles off his jeans and walked slowly back to the house.

9

· Bears? ·

"Where have you been?" asked Mrs. Koota when she saw Jay approaching the house. Without waiting for an answer, she asked, "Have you seen the girls?"

Jay shook his head. "I haven't seen anyone," he said.

"The Horaks left a little while ago," said Aunt Vera. "The girls went off berry picking ages ago. They should be back by now."

Jay was sure the girls would turn up. He wondered where Mickey was—and he wondered how Mickey would treat him now that Roger had pointed out what a baby Jay was.

"Where's Dad?" asked Jay. The Koota's car was not in the driveway.

"Dad wanted to get some more film for his camera," said Mrs. Koota. "He and Uncle Phil drove into town. I wish he was here. I'm worried about the girls."

"They can't be far," said Jay. "They know their way around by now. They're probably off giggling about their secret, whatever it is," he added.

"They've never been gone this long," Aunt Vera insisted. She went into the house and began calling, "Mickey, Mickey."

Mickey came to the door holding a comic book.

"I want you and Jay to go look for the girls," said Aunt Vera.

"Now?" asked Mickey. "Can't I finish this first? Roger gave it to me."

"That comic won't run away," said his

mother. "I'm worried about your sister and Ellen."

Reluctantly, Mickey put down his comic. He turned to Jay. "Come on," he said.

"Now don't you two get lost," called Mrs. Koota as the two boys set off.

"Do you want to split up?" asked Jay. If Mickey didn't want to walk through the woods with a little kid like him, this would give him a way out.

"No," said Mickey. "Let's stick together."

Just a couple of hours ago, Jay thought, Mickey had not wanted to stick with him at all.

The boys walked along the dirt road without talking. Jay thought of the first morning in the woods when he hadn't known what to say to Mickey. "We'd better go down toward the brook," Jay said finally. "That's where the berries grow."

"Your sister probably went looking for a bear," said Mickey.

The boys pushed through the bushes. "A lot of berries grow around here," said Jay.

"I never noticed," said Mickey. "I just eat the pies."

Jay didn't answer. Something tickled his nose and he sneezed.

"There you go again with your sneezes," said Mickey. "Don't forget you promised to teach me how."

Jay had often wondered how he would be able to teach Mickey something that he didn't understand himself. Now he didn't care. All promises were cancelled.

Jay led the way deeper into the woods. "Let's look over there," he said. It was a part of the woods that he knew very well because he had made several houses there. Was it only this afternoon that he had destroyed those houses? It seemed like a long time ago.

The sun was no longer shining through the branches. Instead, it was casting dark shadows all around them.

"It's kind of spooky here, isn't it?" asked Mickey.

Jay looked at Mickey with surprise. He had spent so much time here that it didn't scare him at all. He knew that there were no wild animals behind the bushes. There were bushes behind the bushes, and that was all.

There was still no sign of the girls. Jay

wanted to find a barrette or a sandal or some other clue, the way TV detectives always did. There was nothing. At last the boys decided to go back to the house.

"I bet you anything they are already there," Mickey said. "They're probably eating supper without us."

So the boys turned back and reached the road again. Their fathers were walking toward them.

"Thank goodness we found you. This kind of thing could go on forever," said Uncle Phil. Mickey had been right. The girls were safely back at the house, and the fathers had been sent to look for the boys.

"Ellen and Stacey are very upset," Jay's father said. "They've been crying."

"Did they get hurt?" asked Jay. He had often heard bees buzzing about near the berry bushes.

"They didn't get hurt, but something out in the woods has certainly made them unhappy. It has something to do with elves."

"Elves?" said Mickey.

"It sounds like a game they made up," said Jay.

When they entered the house, both Ellen and Stacey were still crying.

"They're all gone. Not one left," sobbed Ellen.

"What's all gone?" Jay asked his sister. This wasn't one of her silly whines about something being unfair.

"Where are the elves going to live now?" cried Stacey.

"Start from the beginning," said Mrs. Koota. "We don't know what you are talking about."

"We found little elf houses in the woods," said Ellen. "It was our secret. We didn't tell you because we knew you'd say there are no such things as elves."

"But we really saw them," Stacey insisted, "lots of times. They were hidden under bushes and you had to look hard to find them. Probably no other person ever saw them except us. We never touched them. We just looked."

"And this afternoon when we went berry picking, we stopped to look at the houses," Ellen said.

"Only today the houses were all destroyed. We could see the pieces lying all over. Maybe the elves had a war. Maybe all the elves were killed," said Stacey, beginning to cry again.

"Elves don't have wars," said her mother. "You've been listening to too many news broadcasts."

"There are no elves," said Mr. Koota. "It's just your imagination."

"We knew you'd say that. That's why we never told you," sobbed Ellen. "At first I thought maybe a bear had stepped on the houses, but you said there are no bears here."

"Well, if we were wrong about elves, we could be wrong about bears, too," suggested Mrs. Koota.

"Do you think so?" asked Ellen blowing her nose.

Jay couldn't say a word. It was all clear to him now. The girls had found his little houses, and thought they had been built by elves. At another time it would have made him feel great to have fooled the girls. But seeing how upset they both were, he felt awful. If he hadn't destroyed the houses, they would have gone home still believing they had a marvelous secret.

"Hey, listen," he said. "Those weren't elf houses."

"Yes they were!" shouted his sister. "And maybe there are bears here after all. Maybe it was a bear that smashed the houses, so there."

Jay was about to explain that he had made the houses. He was the bear that had destroyed them, too. But then he had a better idea. He would rebuild the houses.

10

· Builders ·

That evening, supper was a quiet meal. No one felt hungry. Stacey and Ellen picked at their food. Jay was worried about how to get out to the woods that night without anyone seeing him. Mickey, too, was unusually quiet.

Jay went to bed without his mother reminding him. Usually he and Mickey would lie in bed trading jokes and riddles long after the lights were turned out. But tonight he and Mickey were no longer the friends they had been the night before and the nights before that. Roger Horak had proven that.

As he lay in bed, Jay began to worry. If he sneaked out into the woods after everyone was asleep, he might not be able to find his way or see what he was doing. Even if he took Mickey's flashlight, it would be impossible to hold it and to build at the same time. Maybe he should wake up early when it just began to get light. But then he probably wouldn't have time to build enough houses.

Jay tossed in his bed. He could hear Mickey tossing in his bed, too. If Mickey helped, I could manage it, he thought. He knew Mickey would laugh at the idea. But he no longer cared. Mickey already thought he was a baby. This would prove it to him, but so what? In another couple of days the vacation would be over. Jay would return to New York and Mickey to Ohio. He could laugh about it with Roger Horak, but it wouldn't matter. Jay wouldn't have to listen to them.

"Mickey?" he whispered.

"Yeah?"

"You know those elf houses that the girls were talking about?"

"Yeah."

"Well, they weren't really built by elves."

"Of course not," said Mickey. "There's no such thing."

"Well," said Jay. "I've seen them."

"You saw some elves?"

"No, stupid," said Jay. "I saw the houses."

"You did? But who could have built them?" asked Mickey.

"I did."

"You?"

"I used to go into the woods sometimes, and I made those little houses. It was my secret, except that the girls found them."

"But who broke them up?" asked Mickey.

"I did," said Jay. "I made them, and I smashed them."

"Wow," said Mickey.

"I didn't know that the girls had found them. And I didn't know they would get so upset. I could tell them that I made them but I have a better idea. I want to rebuild them tomorrow morning very early."

"Can I help?" asked Mickey before Jay could even ask.

"Sure," he said, relieved. "If we got up around six o'clock, we could have them all rebuilt before the girls get up. Then when they went into the woods, they could find them all over again."

Mickey's watch had an alarm attachment. He set it for five forty-five the next morning, but neither boy needed it. They were both awake and busy getting dressed when the beeper on the watch went off. They tiptoed out of the room and out of the house. Jay led the way.

"Why didn't you ever tell me about this before?" Mickey asked as they made their way through the underbrush.

"I was pretty sure you'd think this was a babyish thing to do. I wouldn't have told you now," said Jay, "except that I need help to make them all over again in such a short time." Jay rubbed his arms. It was chilly in the woods so early in the morning.

"I don't care if you want to tell Roger about

this when you get home," Jay continued, "as long as Stacey and Ellen don't find out." He turned his back on Mickey and plunged deeper into the woods.

"Hey, wait up," called Mickey. "Listen," he said, "that was a crummy thing I did yesterday."

Jay turned around and looked at Mickey, but he didn't say anything.

"I mean, Roger is my best friend back home and all," said Mickey. "But I should have told him that you're okay for a kid your size. In fact, most of the time, I don't even remember that you are only eight years old."

Jay didn't trust himself to answer. He was afraid that if he tried to say anything, he would start to cry.

"Anyhow," continued Mickey. "I think you're okay. And if you lived in Ohio, I bet Roger would catch on pretty quick." He paused. "We're still friends, right?"

Jay nodded. "Right," he said. He held out his hand to shake on it.

"We better start," he said to Mickey.

Jay showed Mickey how to anchor twigs in

the ground and use small branches for the rooftops. They made a path using a double row of small pebbles and found moss to line the floor of the house. It was damp in the woods so early in the morning and before long the moisture found its way through both boys' sneakers. But, it didn't bother them as they worked away.

"Here's a good place to build." Mickey showed Jay a crevice between two rocks. "You know, I would never have thought of doing this. But it's fun."

Jay grinned. "The important thing is that Ellen and Stacey never know we made these houses."

"What about our parents?" asked Mickey. "They won't believe it was elves."

"They can think whatever they want," said Jay. "But we won't tell them."

"Right," agreed Mickey. He held out a dirty hand. "Let's shake on it," he said. "I'll never tell a soul as long as I live. Not even Roger." Jay knew Mickey meant it. Mickey wasn't going to tell and neither was he.

By the time Mickey's watch showed seven

forty-five and their stomachs told them it was time for breakfast, fifteen houses had been built in the woods. The boys brushed as much dirt off themselves as possible.

"We better go and change," said Mickey. "If anyone sees us like this, they'll know we were up to something."

"If my mother catches me washing when I took a shower last night, she'll really be suspicious," said Jay. When the boys sat down to breakfast, only the dirt under their fingernails might have given someone a clue about what had gone on at sunrise this morning.

Ellen and Stacey sat quietly at the table.

"Will you show us where the houses used to be?" asked Mickey. "You really should have shared your secret before it was too late."

Ellen's eyes welled up. "I don't want to go to the woods ever again."

"That's enough about elf houses," said Aunt Vera. "I think we should all get into the car and explore some new place today. Why don't we drive to Bennington? There's a museum with paintings by Grandma Moses."

"Good idea," agreed Mrs. Koota.

The girls had to go back to the woods, thought Jay. Otherwise they would never know about the new houses.

When breakfast was finished, Jay took Stacey aside. "Mickey and I will go with you. Please, just show us where the houses were," he said.

"You won't laugh at us?" said Stacey.

"Of course not," said Jay. "We feel we missed something. And maybe we'll be able to figure out what happened to the houses."

Stacey agreed and convinced Ellen to come along. The children retraced the path Jay and Mickey had taken earlier that morning. Mr. Koota came along, too.

"This is where one used to be," said Stacey. Her eyes widened with surprise.

"A house!" she and Ellen shrieked together.

"An elf house!" said Mickey, "just like you said."

"Now you have to believe us," said Ellen.

"I'm going to get my camera," said Mr. Koota.

As the girls walked ahead looking for more houses, Mr. Koota put his arm around Jay.

"That was a thoughtful thing you did," he said to his son.

So his father had guessed. "Don't tell," said Jay looking up at his father.

"Of course not," Mr. Koota agreed.

· 11 ·

· Good-bye to the Woods ·

Without any countdown at all, the vacation in the woods was almost over. But there was still one thing Jay had not yet done. He had not taught Mickey how to sneeze. Mickey was still convinced that Jay could sneeze whenever he wanted to. Jay had let Mickey believe it. But the truth was that sometimes it was a feather from his pillow, sometimes it was pollen from a flower, and sometimes it was a breeze in the air that tickled Jay's nose. It was something that his nose just did and Jay had no control over it. Now Jay had to teach himself the trick of sneezing so that he could teach it to Mickey.

The last evening before they left for home, Jay lay in bed and concentrated on his nose. He ran his finger up and down the outside of his nose to see if that would make him sneeze. It didn't. He wiggled his nostrils and tried to imagine a tickle. He thought of a little feather rubbing against his nose. A tiny sneeze escaped. It was working. A few more practice sneezes and the trick was his.

Jay got a kick out of showing Mickey how to relax his nose. It was like the first day at Snake Lake, when Mickey told Jay to relax his body in the water. Finally, Mickey managed his first little sneeze; and they sneezed happily together that night until they fell asleep.

"All good things must come to an end," said Mr. Koota as they loaded the cars with suitcases and boxes for the trip home. It was just the sort of stupid thing a grownup could be counted on to say, thought Jay. He had only just gotten used to being here, and now it was time to leave already. Jay remembered his first night in the woods. It was only two weeks ago that he and Mickey had gone out looking for a bear.

"It's not fair," said Ellen.

"It's been wonderful," sighed Aunt Vera. "I'm so glad you called us to share this house with you." She was carrying a box with a dozen jars of blackberry jam.

"I've bought a three pound wheel of Vermont cheese," Jay's mother told him. "You can eat sandwiches of this good cheese at home."

"I hope you left some maple syrup for other people," said Mr. Koota to his wife as he carried a bag with several cans out to the car.

It was nice that they were taking all these reminders of the vacation home with them, thought Jay, but it would be better if they could just stay here.

Finally every suitcase and box had been loaded into the two cars. There was lots of hugging and kissing among the adults and the girls. Mickey and Jay didn't say anything.

There didn't seem anything left to say except good-bye. Jay concentrated hard on a sneeze.

"*Aaaaachoooo*," he sneezed loudly, and it made Mickey laugh so hard he couldn't sneeze back.

The parents had all said they wanted to come back next summer. Jay hoped they didn't change their minds.

"What color should I make your sweater?" Aunt Vera asked Jay.

"It's got to be blue for a Jay," said Mickey.

"Well, this is it," said Uncle Phil. The Rosses got into their car and slammed the doors after them.

"Good-bye, good-bye," everyone yelled as the Rosses' car moved slowly down the dirt road.

The Kootas got into their car. "Good-bye," Ellen called out to the house.

Jay sat in the back seat beside his sister. He tried to stay awake so he could watch the woods and mountains as they slid past. His eye lids lowered and popped open again.

"I wish we could have stayed longer," said Ellen sadly. "It was the best summer I ever had."

"School starts the day after tomorrow," Mrs. Koota reminded the children. As if they had forgotten that.

They were going home to all the things they had left behind in the city, thought Jay. But even though they had been gone for only two weeks, Jay knew he had changed. He wondered what fourth grade would be like for the *new* Jay.

He was a boy who had climbed a mountain three times, learned to swim (almost), lost five pounds on the scale in the upstairs bathroom, been brave enough to catch a bat, and made two new friends: Mickey and Stacey. If he could do all that in just two weeks, what could he do in a full year in fourth grade!